Dear Parent:
Your child's love of reading starts here!

Every child learns to read in a different way and at his or her own speed. Some go back and forth between reading levels and read favorite books again and again. Others read through each level in order. You can help your young reader improve and become more confident by encouraging his or her own interests and abilities. From books your child reads with you to the first books he or she reads alone, there are I Can Read Books for every stage of reading:

SHARED READING
Basic language, word repetition, and whimsical illustrations, ideal for sharing with your emergent reader

BEGINNING READING
Short sentences, familiar words, and simple concepts for children eager to read on their own

READING WITH HELP
Engaging stories, longer sentences, and language play for developing readers

READING ALONE
Complex plots, challenging vocabulary, and high-interest topics for the independent reader

I Can Read Books have introduced children to the joy of reading since 1957. Featuring award-winning authors and illustrators and a fabulous cast of beloved characters, I Can Read Books set the standard for beginning readers.

A lifetime of discovery begins with the magical words **"I Can Read!"**

Visit www.icanread.com for information
on enriching your child's reading experience.

To Will's naptime

Balzer + Bray is an imprint of HarperCollins Publishers.
I Can Read® and I Can Read Book® are trademarks of HarperCollins Publishers.

Fox at Night
Copyright © 2021 by Corey R. Tabor
All rights reserved. Printed in the United States of America.
No part of this book may be used or reproduced in any manner whatsoever without written permission except
in the case of brief quotations embodied in critical articles and reviews. For information address HarperCollins
Children's Books, a division of HarperCollins Publishers, 195 Broadway, New York, NY 10007.
www.icanread.com

ISBN 978-0-06-297708-3 (trade bdg.) — ISBN 978-0-06-297707-6 (pbk.)

The artist used pencil, colored pencil, and watercolor, assembled digitally, to create the illustrations for this
book.
Typography by Dana Fritts
Title hand lettering by Alexandra Snowdon

22 CWM 10 9 8 7 6 5   ❖ First Edition

My First
SHARED READING

I Can Read!

FOX at NIGHT

Corey R. Tabor

BALZER + BRAY

An Imprint of HarperCollinsPublishers

It is night, and
Fox is scared.

"The night is full

of monsters," says Fox.

Fox looks for monsters.

Fox sees four stars.

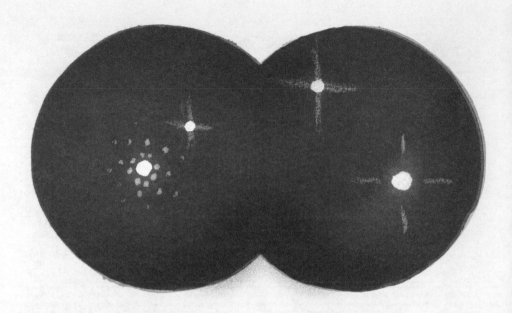

Fox sees three planets.

Fox sees two big wings.

Fox sees two big pointy ears.

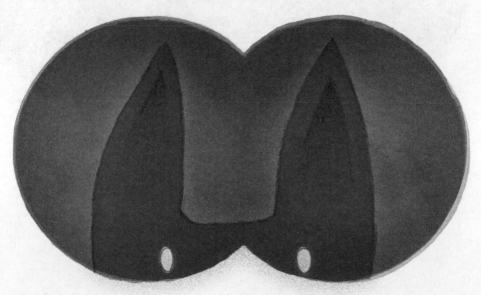

Fox sees two

big yellow eyes.

"Monster!" cries Fox.

"I am not a monster.

I am a bat," says Bat.

"Sorry," says Fox. "But the night

is full of monsters."

"I don't think so," says Bat.

"Come, I will show you."

Fox and Bat go out
into the night.

Fox hears a TAP TAP TAP.

Fox hears a

BOOM BOOM BANG.

"Monster!" cries Fox.

"I am not a monster. I am a raccoon,"
says Raccoon.

"Sorry," says Fox. "But the night is full of monsters."

"I don't think so," says Raccoon. "Come, we will show you."

Fox smells a stink.

Fox smells a big
awful stink.

"Monster!" cries Fox.

"I am not a monster.

I am a skunk," says Skunk.

"Sorry," says Fox. "But the night

is full of monsters."

"I don't think so," says Skunk.

"Come, we will show you."

Fox sees two pointy horns.

Fox sees three yellow eyes.

Fox sees lots of pointy teeth.

"Monsters!" cries the tiny

little monster.

"I told you," says Fox. "The night is full of monsters."